For my sister, Susanna.

Special thanks to Claudia and Philip Davis

Published in 2016 by Little Boo Publishing

ISBN: 978-0-9934203-6-8

From the author of **Paddy and the Magic Pirate Hat**, **Bea Gives Up Her Pacifier**,
and **Tell Me About Heaven, Grandpa Rabbit!**,
winner of the *Gold Prima Baby Award* for *Best Children's Book.*

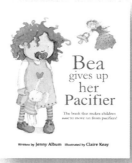

little boo publishing

Ben gives up his Pacifier

Written by **Jenny Album**   Illustrated by **Claire Keay**

little boo publishing

Ben had a pacifier,
which he used ALL the time.

He used it in the day when he played…

He used it in the night when
he went to sleep…

And sometimes, he even
used it in the bath.

Then, one day, Mommy said, "Ben, you're far too old to use a pacifier now. They're for little babies, not children as old as you."

"Also, pacifiers make your teeth stick out, so if you're not careful, you might start to look like a bunny rabbit."

Ben imagined what he would look like as a
bunny rabbit – and he didn't like it very
much.

Also, it was true what Mommy had said.
He *was* the only one of his friends who still
used a pacifier.

"So what shall I do Mommy?" asked Ben.
"Give them to the Pacifier Fairy of course!"
Mommy replied.

So the next day Ben and Mommy went round the
house and collected up all of his pacifiers.

They found a pacifier at the bottom
of the toy box…

They found a pacifier
under the sofa cushions…

They even found a pacifier
underneath the piano.
(It was very dusty.)

That night Ben put all the pacifiers in a big brown
envelope and left it outside his
bedroom door.

Mommy told Ben that if he was a good boy
and went straight to sleep with a smile on
his face, he might receive something special
from the Pacifier Fairy the next day…

So, with a happy little smile Ben drifted off to sleep.

Later that night, Ben woke up to see a tiny fairy
sitting on his lampshade.

"Hello," said the fairy,
"I'm the Pacifier Fairy, and I've come to
take all of your pacifiers off to Fairyland."

"Why?" said Ben.

"Well," she replied, "we fairies have lots
of uses for pacifiers…"

"Sometimes we use them as boats
to sail down the river."

"And the fairy children use them as merry-go-rounds to spin round and round in the fairy playground."

"And when the weather's really bad in Fairyland, some fairies use them as umbrellas to shelter from the rain."

"Wow!" said Ben. "I didn't know that!"

Then he paused. "But Pacifier Fairy…" he said.
"I know the fairies really need my pacifiers,
and I do want them to have them. But…er…
I still *really* want my pacifier too!"

Gently the Pacifier Fairy said, "Don't worry Ben, every time you start to miss your pacifier, just think very hard about something you love to eat. If you do, I will magically make you *taste* that special thing in your mouth."

Then she waved her magic wand and Ben went straight to sleep.

When he woke up, the envelope outside his door had gone. And in its place was a little present from the Pacifier Fairy!

Ben was very happy.

That day, Ben didn't really miss his pacifier at all.
But that night, when he went to bed, he did a bit.

So as he lay there, Ben decided to think very hard
about honey on hot buttered toast.

And guess what? Suddenly he could actually
taste the honey in his mouth.

The next night when he missed his
pacifier he thought about a thick, creamy
banana smoothie!

And the next night, he thought of…well he
didn't think of anything very much really…
he just fell straight to sleep.

In the corner of the room a little fairy smiled
and waved goodbye.

Her magic was done…

Made in United States
North Haven, CT
08 October 2022

25192968R00015